7years before Hashiu

This book
belongs to

Hashim

Mahis

7 years later

Hasham.c

Munsch Mania!

A Robert Munsch Collection

Illustrated by

Michael Martchenko

and

Jay Odjick

Scholastic Canada Ltd.
Toronto New York London Auckland Sydney
Mexico City New Delhi Hong Kong Buenos Aires

www.scholastic.ca

Library and Archives Canada Cataloguing in Publication

Munsch, Robert N., 1945-
[Novels. Selections]
    Munsch mania! : a Robert Munsch collection / by Robert Munsch ; illustrated
by Michael Martchenko and Jay Odjick ; translations by Christiane Duchesne and
Rose Trudeau.

Contents: I'm so embarrassed! -- No clean clothes -- Class clown -- Look at
    me! -- Just one goal!
Includes some text in French and Ojibwa.
ISBN 978-1-4431-2826-1 (bound)

    1. Children's stories, Canadian. I. Duchesne, Christiane, 1949- II. Munsch,
Robert N., 1945- I'm so embarrassed! III. Title. IV. Title: Novels. Selections.

PS8576.U575A6 2013   jC813'.54   C2013-902388-7

6 5 4 3 2 1   Printed in China 38   13 14 15 16 17

Contents

*To Lacey Clarke
Stewart, British Columbia.*
— R.M.

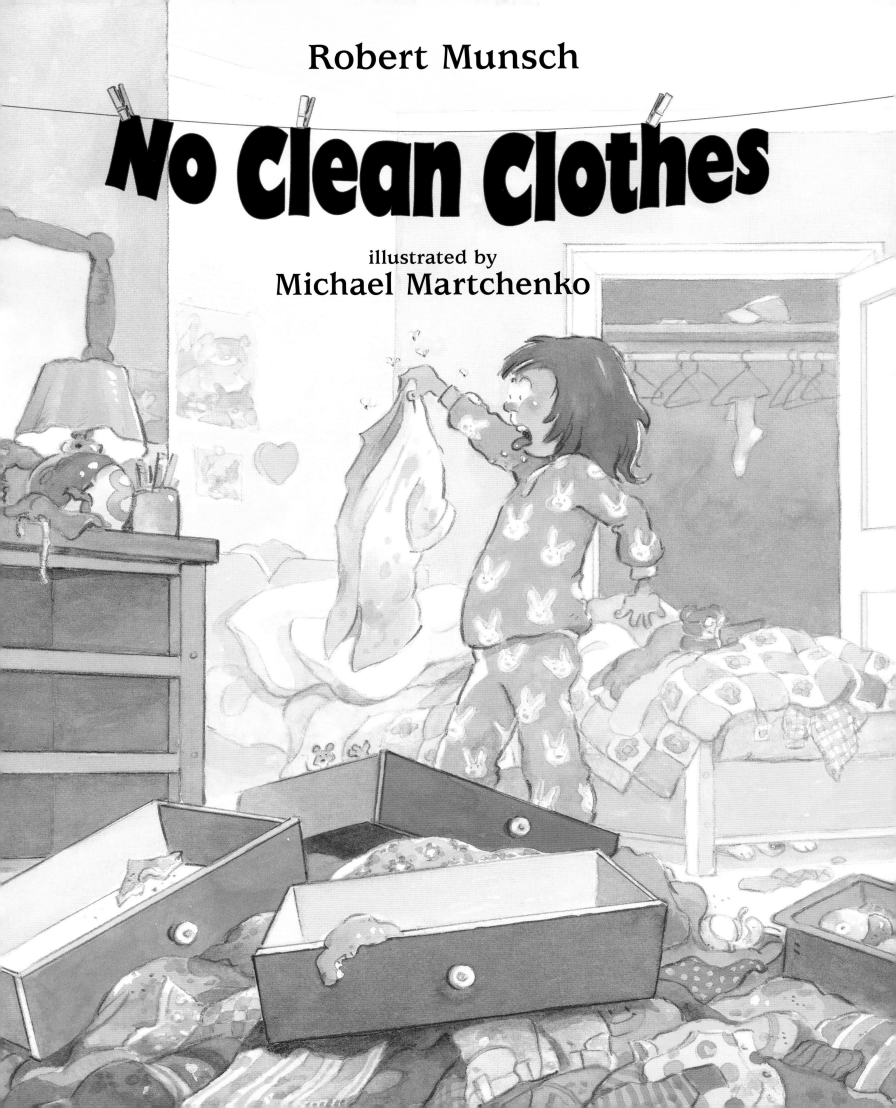

Lacey opened the top drawer of her dresser:

NO CLEAN CLOTHES!

Lacey opened the middle drawer of her dresser:

NO CLEAN CLOTHES!

Lacey opened the bottom drawer of her dresser:

NO CLEAN CLOTHES!

Lacey looked all around her bedroom:

NO CLEAN CLOTHES!

She ran downstairs and yelled, "Mom! Mom! Mom! Why didn't you wash my clothes?"

"Lacey," said her mother, "I would WASH your clothes if I could FIND your clothes!

"You hide them under your bed!

"You lend them to your friends!

"You leave them in the backyard!

"Sometimes I think you feed your underwear to the dog!"

"Mom," said Lacey, "don't be silly! All I need is one shirt. Can't you find me just one clean shirt?"

"Well," said her mom, "there is that nice shirt that Grandma gave you for your birthday. You have never worn it."

"That shirt is a Strange Grandma Present," said Lacey.

"When I was three, Grandma gave me a shirt that said SNOOGIE WOOKUMS, and everyone laughed at me.

"When I was four, Grandma gave me a shirt that said CUTIE PATOOTIE, and everyone laughed at me."

"When I was five, Grandma gave me a shirt that said CUDDLY WUNKUMS, and everyone laughed at me.

"Now I am six, and Grandma gives me a shirt that says KISS ME — I'M PERFECT. I am NOT wearing that shirt to school. Only a grandma would choose a shirt like that."

"Now Lacey," said her mom, "just wear it for this morning. I will wash a shirt and bring it to school at recess."

"You will wash it right away?" said Lacey.

"Yes," said Lacey's mom.

"You will not talk on the phone?"

"No," said her mom.

"You will not wash the dishes?"

"No," said her mom.

"You will not go shopping on the way?"

"No," said her mom.

"You will not go to work and chop down a tree?"

"No," said her mom.

"OK!" said Lacey. "I will be on the steps of the school at recess."

Lacey put on the Strange Grandma Shirt and walked down the road. A kitty cat looked up at her, read her shirt, and gave her a kitty cat kiss on her ear:

Lick — Lick — Lick — Lick — Lick — Lick

"Neat!" said Lacey. "I got a kitty-cat kiss. Maybe I am going to like this shirt."

She walked farther down the street
and met a dog.

The dog read Lacey's shirt,
jumped up, and gave her a doggy
kiss on the ear:

Sphlick — Sphlick — Sphlick

"WOW!" said Lacey. "I got a
kitty-cat kiss and a doggy kiss! This is
a wonderful shirt!"

Lacey walked farther down the street. An eagle flew in circles around her and landed on her head. It leaned down, read her shirt, and gave her an eagle kiss on the nose:

DINK — DINK — DINK

Lacey yelled, "An eagle kiss! An eagle kiss! I got an eagle kiss! I love my grandma! I love this shirt!"

Lacey walked farther down
the street and met a moose.

The moose looked at Lacey, read her shirt, and gave her a large wet moose kiss right up the front of her face and over the top of her head:

SPHLURRRRRRRRRRRRCHHHHH

"Fantastic!" said Lacey. "I am the first person ever to be kissed by a moose."

When Lacey got to school, she ran inside and yelled, "Teacher! Teacher! Look! I got a kitty-cat kiss. I got a doggy kiss. I got an eagle kiss. I got a moose kiss — all because of my Wonderful Grandma Shirt!"

"Neat," said her teacher. "But maybe you should go and wash. Your hair is full of green moose slime."

"Yuck!" said Lacey. "Very gross!"

When Lacey came back to her desk, a boy named Johnny sat down beside her. He read her shirt and gave her a kiss.

"GWAAAAACHHHHK!"

yelled Lacey.

"BOY KISS! AHHHHHHH!"

She ran back into the bathroom and washed her face until recess. Then she went back outside and got really lucky because she was kissed . . .

BY A BEAR!

When Lacey got home after school her mother said, "I didn't see you at school. Did Grandma's shirt turn out to be OK?"

"I love it," said Lacey. "And I called Grandma from the principal's office. She's going to send everyone at school a Strange Grandma Shirt."

No Clean Clothes

In 1988 Scholastic held a contest where I was the prize. The class that wrote the best invitation would win me. Lots of classes from all over Canada entered the contest and I ended up being won by a Grade 2 class from Stewart, British Columbia. I thought it was really neat that Stewart was an isolated town at the end of a long, dead-end road that was often closed by avalanches.

I made up three stories while I was there, and almost got killed by an avalanche. *No Clean Clothes* was one of the stories. It happened because a kid named Lacey came to school wearing a shirt that said "Kiss Me! I'm Perfect."

Since the school could not go out for recess because there were three grizzly bears on the playground, I made up a story about Lacey walking to school and getting kissed by lots of the local animals like bears and wolves and moose and caribou (NEAT!) and finally by a boy (YUCK!). When the book was published, Lacey was 15 and lived in Smithers, B.C. I went to her high school and had a book launch party. Lacey invited a lot of little kids to the high school, so I did a big storytelling to little kids and high school kids at the same time.

All the buildings in the book are real buildings from Stewart, B.C. Michael Martchenko also hid an elephant in the book. Michael is definitely going crazy. There are LOTS of animals in Stewart, but I did not see any elephants.

For Leonardo Gomez-Varela
San Antonio, Texas
— R.M.

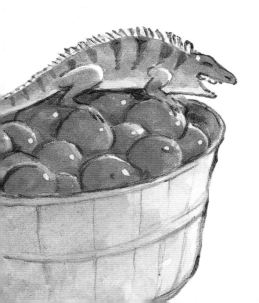

ROBERT MUNSCH
Class Clown

ILLUSTRATED BY
MICHAEL
MARTCHENKO

When Leonardo was a baby, his mother laughed all the time. She said, "This baby is *sooooo* funny!"

When Leonardo was one year old, his grandma and grandpa laughed all the time. They said, "This baby is *sooooo* funny!"

When Leonardo was three years old, EVERYONE laughed. They said, "This kid is *sooooo* funny!"

When Leonardo was in Grade One,
the kids laughed all the time. They
said, "Leonardo is *sooooo* funny!
He is our class clown."

But Mrs. Gomez said, "Leonardo, you have to stop! The kids are laughing all the time, and nobody is learning. STOP BEING FUNNY!"

"OK," said Leonardo, and for the first time in his whole life, he stopped being funny.

After one minute, Leonardo felt really strange.

After two minutes, he felt a little bit sick.

After three minutes, he started to chew his fingernails.

After four minutes, he started to rock back and forth in his seat.

After five minutes, he said, "I know that Mrs. Gomez is really tired of me being the class clown, but I just HAVE to do something funny."

So Leonardo looked at the girl sitting next to him and made a funny face.

The girl didn't do anything.

So Leonardo made a really funny face,
and the girl laughed so hard she fell off
her chair and rolled around on the floor.
"Stop!" said Mrs. Gomez.
But the girl kept laughing.

"STOP!" yelled Mrs. Gomez, and finally the girl stopped laughing and got back in her seat.

"What is going on?" said Mrs. Gomez to the girl.

"I was thinking of something very funny," said the girl.

"No thinking in my class," said Mrs. Gomez.

"OK," said the girl. "I will never think again."

"Good!" said Mrs. Gomez.

Leonardo couldn't stop. He said,
"I know that Mrs. Gomez is really, really
tired of me being the class clown, and
I will probably get in big trouble, but
I just HAVE to do something else funny."

So Leonardo leaned over to the boy
next to him and told a funny joke.

The boy didn't do anything.

So Leonardo leaned over again and told a really, really funny joke, and the boy laughed so hard he fell off his chair, rolled around on the floor and kicked over his desk.

"Stop!" said Mrs. Gomez.

The boy kept rolling around on the floor.

"STOP!" yelled Mrs. Gomez. "What is going on?"

"I remembered something very funny," said the boy.

"Well, don't remember anything in my class," said Mrs. Gomez.

"OK," said the boy. "I will never remember anything again."

"Good!" said Mrs. Gomez.

Leonardo was OK till after lunch. Then he said, "I know that Mrs. Gomez is really, really, really tired of me being the class clown, and I will probably get in big trouble, but I just HAVE to do one last funny thing."

So while Mrs. Gomez was writing on the chalkboard, Leonardo drew a funny picture and held it up so everyone could see it.

Nobody laughed.

So Leonardo drew a really, really, REALLY funny picture, held it up, and all the kids in the class laughed so hard they fell off their chairs, rolled around on the floor and knocked over their desks.

"STOP!" yelled Mrs. Gomez. "What's going on?"

"It's Leonardo!" all the kids yelled. "He's being the class clown."

"Leonardo," said Mrs. Gomez, "I have told you to stop being a clown, and now I am getting really, really, REALLY mad!"

"OK!" said Leonardo. "I will never, ever be funny again."

"HA!" said Mrs. Gomez, and she laughed so hard she fell down, rolled around on the floor and kicked over her desk.

She said, "Leonardo, you are *sooooo* funny!"

And that was when Leonardo decided that when he grew up, he was going to be . . .

A CLOWN!

About Class Clown

In 2005, Two kids named Ricky and Drew from Ed Cody Elementary School sent me a movie that they had made themselves. It was a show about why I should visit San Antonio. I thought it was really neat that they had made it themselves, and I decided to visit the school.

After lots of other neat stuff, like Mexican dancers and wonderful Mexican food (and not-so-wonderful food like "cowboy stew," which was cow guts), I went to Mrs. Gomes's class which was all in Spanish and they tried to teach me the states of Mexico.

They had made me an excellent map, which I got to keep. They made me a Spanish ABC book, which I got to keep. They even made me a song about the states of Mexico so I could learn how to say the names right.

When all this wonderful stuff was over, I told some stories and then answered questions. A kid named Leonardo asked, "How do you get your ideas?"

I said, "I'll show you." So I asked the other kids to talk to me about Leonardo till I got an idea for a story. Usually this leads to an interesting conversation about the kid, but not this time. The whole class yelled in unison, "CLASS CLOWN!" Right then I made up the story.

It was all a question of asking the right question about the right kid. The moment they said "class clown," I realized that everybody knew what a class clown was, and every class has a class clown, and I did not have a class clown story.

Robert Munsch

Illustrated by Michael Martchenko

Just One Goal!

"A rink! A rink! A rink!" said Ciara to her father. "A rink on the river would be nice. I would not have to go all the way across town to play hockey."

"The ice on the river is a mess!" said her father. "It froze all jagged and bumpy. We can't make a rink."

"A rink! A rink! A rink!" said Ciara to her mother. "A rink on the river would be nice. I would not have to go all the way across town to play hockey."

"Too bumpy!" said her mother. "The river ice is too bumpy to make into a rink."

"A rink! A rink! A rink!" said Ciara to her sisters. "A rink on the river would be nice. I could walk right out the back door and down to the river and play on my own rink."

"Well, WE had to go across town to play hockey," said Ciara's sisters, "and that was good enough for us. So YOU have to go across town just like WE did."

"OK, OK, OK!" said Ciara.

She got a glass of warm water and a spoon, and went across the backyard, down the hill, to the frozen bumpy river. She used the water and the spoon to make a very small hockey rink — a good hockey rink for ants.

Ciara spent the whole next day
carrying warm water down to the river.
She worked till it was dark and the
Northern Lights came out.

Finally her rink was big enough for
a small dog.

Ciara's dad came looking for her
and said, "Wow! A rink! You really made
a rink."

"And I am just a little kid!" said Ciara.

The next day Ciara's dad rented a bulldozer and flattened a lot of river ice. Then all the neighbours came down and helped. By the time the Northern Lights came out, there was a real, people-sized rink on the river.

"A rink! A rink! A rink!" yelled Ciara. "A real rink on the river and now we do not have to go all the way across town to play hockey."

Ciara started skating and did not go to bed at all that night.

The next day, Ciara put up a sign that said "RIVER RATS RINK" and lots of kids came to play. But no matter what side Ciara was on, her team always lost.

One game that Ciara might have won ended when a moose went to sleep in the net.

Another game ended when a bear
chased everyone off the ice.

Another game ended when a bunch
of teenagers raced through on their
snowmobiles.

And that is why Ciara's team did not want to end a tied game just because the ice was a little wet. It was Ciara's last chance to win a game that year.

But suddenly, the rink started floating
down the river while the rest of the ice
crashed and boomed around it.

The players did not even notice.

Ciara's mom noticed.

"AHHHHHHHHHHH!" yelled Ciara's
mom. "BREAKUP!"

She ran along the river yelling "STOP! STOP! STOP!" but the players could not hear because the ice was making so much noise.

Ciara's father ran along the river yelling "STOP! STOP! STOP!" but the players could not hear because the ice was making so much noise.

Then all the parents ran along the river yelling "STOP! STOP! STOP!" but the teams just kept playing.

"The bridge!" yelled Ciara's mom. "We can catch them at the bridge!"

Everyone jumped into their cars and drove to the bridge. Then the dads hung from the bridge and the moms hung from the dads and the moms grabbed their kids as the rink went floating by.

But nobody got Ciara. She had the puck and was skating very fast toward the goal.

Ciara's dad ran to his car, got his fishing rod, and cast his hook way, way, way down the river.

He caught Ciara just as she scored.
"WE WIN!" yelled Ciara's team,
and all the moms and dads fainted.

Then the kids carried their moms
and dads to a restaurant and fed them hot
chocolate while Ciara planned . . .
NEXT YEAR'S RINK!

Just One Goal!

While I was in in Hay River, Northwest Territories, in 2004, I decided to visit Fort Resolution, a 270-kilometre drive along a mostly dirt road. A guy in Hay River named Brad Mapes lent me his 4-wheel-drive truck for the trip (and it was really nice that I had a 4-wheel-drive vehicle!) When I returned it, Ciara, Brad's daughter, was just back from playing hockey across town. I asked why there was no rink in the river in back of the house. That led to this story, which is the best story I made up on this trip.

I stayed with four families to get story ideas, but the best story came from an accidental meeting just as the trip was ending!

Another neat thing about this book is that it has been translated into Inuktitut.

*To Andrew Livingston and
Taylor Jae Gordon,
Cobalt, Ontario.*
— R.M.

I'M SO EMBARRASSED!

Robert Munsch   Michael Martchenko

"Andrew," said his mom, "let's go to the mall. You need some new shoes."

"NO!" said Andrew. "You always embarrass me when we go to the mall. You always say you are *not* going to embarrass me and you always *do*, so NO! I am not going to the mall."

"I promise not to embarrass you," said his mom.

"HA!" said Andrew, but he went anyway,
because he really needed to get new shoes.

Just at the door to the mall, Andrew's mother said, "Oh, Andrew! You didn't comb your hair."

So Andrew's mother spit on her hand and patted Andrew's hair till it was all flat.

"AHHHHH!" yelled Andrew. "*Spit!* Mommy-spit on my hair at the mall! *Very embarrassing!*"

"Oh, dear!" said Andrew's mom. "I am sorry about the spit. I keep forgetting how big you are. Don't worry. I will be very careful and will not embarrass you again."

"HA!" said Andrew.

So Andrew and his mom went
walking down the mall, and Andrew
saw his aunt.

"Please! Please!" said Andrew.
"Don't say hello to my kissy aunt."

"Oh, Andrew," said his mom.
"I have to say hello."

So Andrew's mom said hello, and
Andrew's aunt gave him a big *hug*

SCRUNCH

and a large wet *kiss*

spHLUrt

that left lipstick all over his face.

"**GWACKHH!**" yelled
Andrew. "Lipstick hugs and kisses!
Lipstick hugs and kisses at the mall!
I think I am going to die."

Andrew hid up in a tree.

Andrew's mom talked to his aunt for about three hours, and then she said, "Andrew? Where are you? Don't get lost. Why are you up in a tree?"

"I am definitely going to get lost if I don't stop getting hugs and kisses," said Andrew.

"Hugs are nice," said his mom.
"GWACKHH!" said Andrew.

They walked some more, and Andrew saw his teacher.

"Please," said Andrew. "Please, please, *please* do not let my mom say hi to my teacher."

But his mom yelled, *"Hello, Andrew's Teacher!* Andrew says you are his best teacher ever, and we are so happy that he got you for a teacher, and would you like to see some of Andrew's baby pictures?"

"AHHHHH!" yelled Andrew. "Baby pictures! AHHHHHH!"

"Andrew," said his mom, "stand beside your teacher. I am going to take a picture."

Andrew ran away. His mom found him and said, "Andrew, why are you hiding behind a trash can?"

"Baby pictures!" said Andrew. "You showed baby pictures to my teacher. Very embarrassing! You promised you were not going to embarrass me."

"OK! OK! OK!" said his mom. "I will be very careful and I will not embarrass you any more. I'm sorry. I'm sorry."

"Look," said Andrew. "There is Taylor-Jae from my school. How about I stay with Taylor-Jae, and you go shop by yourself for a while."

"Good idea," said Andrew's mom.

"Taylor-Jae," said Andrew. "I am going nuts. My mom is embarrassing me all over the place. I am glad you are here, so my mom will leave me alone."

"Maybe you should not be so glad," said Taylor-Jae. "Here comes *my* mom!"

Taylor-Jae's mom came up and said, "Taylor-Jae, do you want me to buy the pink underpants or the yellow underpants?"

"AHHHHHH!" yelled Taylor-Jae. "Underpants in a boy's face!"

Andrew and Taylor-Jae ran across the mall and jumped into a trash can.

After a while their moms came
by and knocked on the trash can.
"Andrew," said his mom, "why
are you in the trash can?"

"I am here because I am so embarrassed," said Andrew.

"Me too!" said Taylor-Jae.

"I don't believe it. Underpants in a boy's face!"

"Now, now!" said their moms. "You're just too sensitive. You should not let things bother you so much."

"OK," said Andrew and Taylor-Jae. "Then this won't bother you!"

They jumped out of the trash can, ran into the middle of the mall and yelled, "Our moms snore like grizzly bears and blame it on our dads!"

Both moms yelled, "AHHHHHH!" and jumped into the trash can.

Andrew and Taylor-Jae knocked on the trash can and their moms yelled, "How could you embarrass us so?"

"Well," said Andrew and Taylor-Jae, "WE HAD GOOD TEACHERS!"

I'M SO EMBARRASSED!

A lot of schools ask me to visit. Mrs. Livingston's class at St. Patrick School in Cobalt, Ontario sent me one of the best invitations.

Her class to wrote me in Grade 3. They sent me a book, which I put on my website, in Grade 4. They wrote again in Grade 7 to say that it was my last chance to visit — so I did.

When I got to the North Bay airport, Mrs. Livingston met me to drive me to Cobalt. In the car were her son, Andrew, and a bunch of the other kids from Grade 7. At the airport, I noticed how embarrassed Andrew was when his mom gave me a hug. In the car I asked him what his mom did to embarrass him and he gave me this list:

1. Talks too much to people she meets.
2. Hugs people.
3. Tells people stories about when he was a baby.
4. Takes pictures all the time.

To which I added:

5. Wears weird clothes.

While I was there, I stayed with Taylor Jae, who lives right on the north end of Lake Temiskaming.

For Madison Snow,
Orangeville, Ontario.
— R.M.

Robert Munsch
Look at Me!

Illustrated by
Michael Martchenko

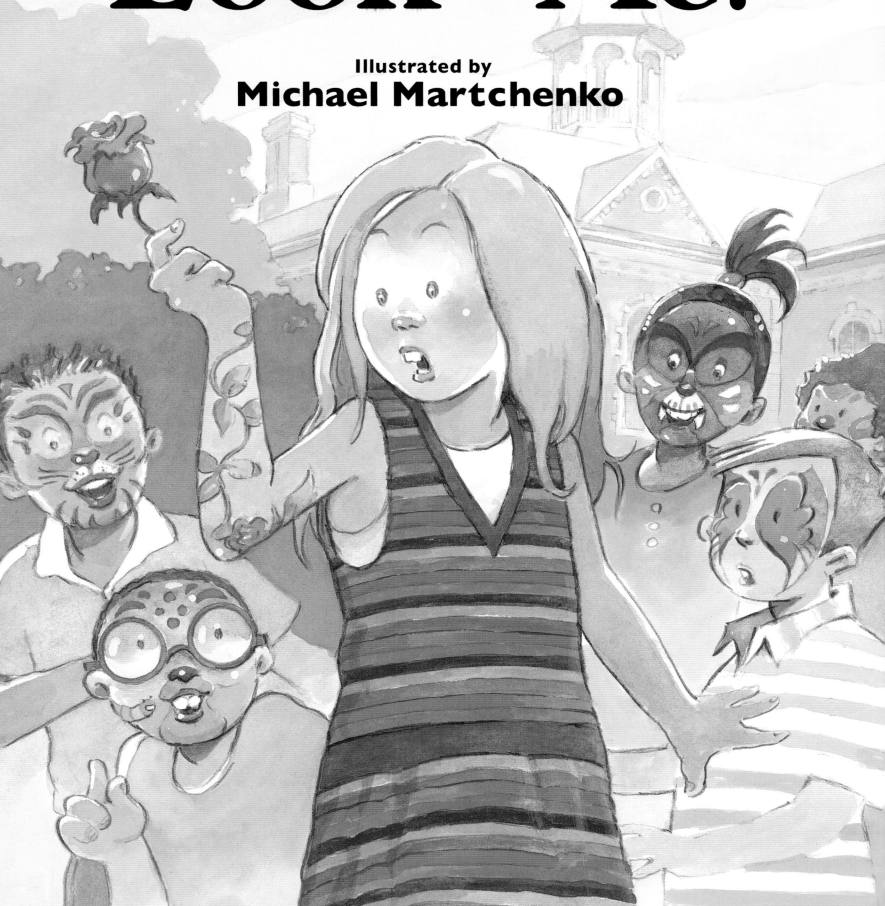

When Madison's grandma came to visit, everyone decided to go for a walk downtown.

In front of city hall, Madison said, "Look! Look! Look! I found a ticket — a ticket for free face painting at the park."

"Neat," said Madison's grandma. "Let's go to the park."

At the park, Madison got in a long, long line.

A girl came and said, "Get a scary face like mine."

"No," said Madison.

A boy came and said, "Get a tiger face like mine."

"No," said Madison.
A girl came and said, "Get a butterfly face like mine."
"NO," said Madison.

Finally it was Madison's turn.

"I want," said Madison, "just on my cheek, a small, perfect rose that looks really real."

"Really real?" said the face painter.

"Really real!" said Madison, and the face painter spent a long, long time painting a small, perfect rose that looked really real.

"That's a nice flower," said Madison's dad. "Now let's go look in some stores."

At the hardware store, when her father was looking at drills and saws, Madison whispered, "Daddy! I think my flower is growing."

"That's nice," said her father.

"Daddy," whispered Madison.
"Look! Look! Look! Please really
LOOK at me. My flower is growing!
There was just one rose, and now
there are two."

Madison's father looked very closely at Madison's face and said, "Why, there really *are* two roses, one on each cheek! But I think it was that way already."

At the kitchen store, when her mother was looking at pots and pans, Madison said, "Mommy! My flower is growing."

"That's nice," said Madison's mother.

"Mommy," said Madison. "Look! Look! Look! Please really LOOK at me! My flower is growing! There was just one rose, and now there are three."

Madison's mother looked very closely at Madison's face and said, "Why, there *are* three roses! I thought you just asked for one."

"I did ask for one rose," said Madison.

"Well, I guess that face painter gave you three," said Madison's mother.

At the ice cream shop, Madison said, "Grandma! My flower is growing."

"That's nice," said Madison's grandma.

"Grandma!" said Madison. "Look! Look! Look! Please really LOOK at me! My flower is growing! There was one rose, and now there are twenty-four . . . and I think a leaf is growing out my ear!"

Then Madison turned over her arms. Ten roses were going down each arm, and while her grandma looked, another rose grew on the end of each stem.

"One rose was nice," said Madison. "Twenty-six is too many."

"This is serious!" said Madison's grandma, and she picked up Madison and ran down the street to the doctor's office.

The doctor was no help. She said, "I know a lot about people, but not a lot about plants."

"Let's try the garden store," said Madison.

At the garden store, the man behind the counter said, "Weed poison! Check out our Wonderful Weed Whomper!"

"AAAAAAAAAAAAHHHHHHHHH!"
yelled Madison. "No Weed Whomper."

"I know," said Madison. "Let's be nice to the rose. I will go home and take a nap with a large flower pot beside my bed, and maybe the rose will go and live in the flower pot."

When Madison
woke up, there was
a huge rose bush
in the flower pot,
and just one perfect
rose on her cheek.
Madison's grandma
took the rose bush
home and planted
it in her garden,
where it stayed until
it found a better
place to grow.

Look at Me!

This is really simple. I met Madison and her mother at the Easter Seals Telethon. I had been volunteered to take part by Lauretta Reid, the kid who is in *Zoom*. I was on TV for 10 hours!

Madison was there with a flower painted on her cheek, and she took care of my coat when I was on TV. I made up this story for her on the spot. I made up lots of stories there and this was the one that I liked the best. Later I visited her school to tell it to her class.

Look at Me! takes place in Madison's hometown of Orangeville, Ontario and all the action takes place on the main street. The next year at the telethon, Madison had a butterfly painted on her face. She asked me how the story was doing. I told her I was telling it a lot and that it was going to be a book.

For Vincent, Port Simpson, B.C., and to all
Anishinaabe Language Learners.
— RM

Gchi Miigwech to: Robert Munsch

This book is different from most of Robert Munsch's books. It is not a funny story: it is a story about growing up and about losing a family member. And it was first published not in English or French, but in Anishinaabemowin, the language spoken by the Anishinaabe people.

The book's original publisher says: "Mr. Munsch's generosity made our project possible. His dedication to helping children all over the world is inspiring, and we are thankful for the opportunity to use his work in our efforts to retain and revitalize the Anishinaabemowin language. His global popularity among children demonstrates his ability to transcend cultural differences — his stories demonstrate our similarities through shared childhood experiences. Jay Odjick did an amazing job, and his artwork appropriately reflected both Mr. Munsch's style and the Anishinaabe people."

We would like to thank the creators of this book for allowing us to include it here, complete with its original artwork by Anishinaabe artist Jay Odjick, Anishinaabemowin translation and syllable chart.

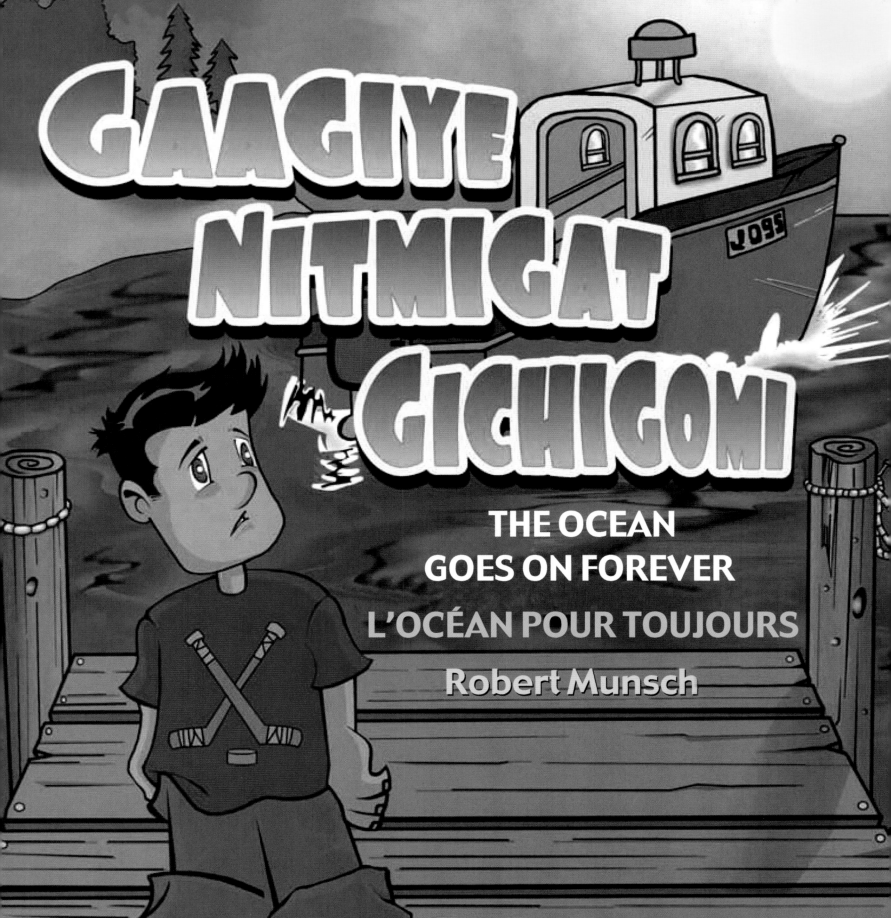

GAAGIYE NITMIGAT GICHIGOMI

**THE OCEAN
GOES ON FOREVER**

L'OCÉAN POUR TOUJOURS

Robert Munsch

illustrations
Jay Odjick

My father and uncle went fishing for salmon, but they didn't take me. I was too little.

Mon père et mon oncle sont partis pêcher le saumon, mais ils ne m'ont pas emmené. Je suis trop petit.

Gaawiin ngii maajiingoosiik noos miinawaa nzhizhenh pii gii bibaa nimeksike'aat. Ozaam ngii gaachiiw.

I was not too little to figure out that the clown who came to our school was not a real clown. I pulled off his wig, and he had regular black hair underneath. The principal didn't like that at all.

Je ne suis pas trop petit pour comprendre que le clown qui est venu à notre école n'est pas un vrai clown. J'ai tiré sur sa perruque. Dessous, il avait des cheveux noirs ordinaires. Le directeur n'a pas aimé ça du tout.

Gaawiin dash wiyii go ozaam ngii gaachiiwisii wii gikenimak giyegeti gii aawisik owo e baapizhiwet pii gii bizhaat wodi kinoomaagegamigoong. Gii makadewaanoon miinjisan pii e naankibidomowak iwi miinjisekaajigan dibaang. Gaawiin gii bishigendaziin owo kinoomaagegamigoong naagaanizit pii e zhichige yaanh iwi.

I was not too little to figure out that the principal also wore a wig. I pulled it off when he walked under the blackboard. The principal did not like that.

Je ne suis pas trop petit pour comprendre que le directeur porte une perruque lui aussi. J'ai tiré dessus quand il est allé au tableau. Il n'a pas aimé ça du tout.

Gaawiin sa gonaa ozaam ngii gaachiiwisii wii gikenimak owo kinoomaagegamigoong naagaanizit gewiin biiskong miinjisekaajigan. Epiichi damino'aanh mkade-bsagaagwong ngii naankibidomowaa iwi miinjisekaajigan pii bemset zhewe. Gaawiin gii bishigendaziin owo kinoomaagemamigoong naagaanizit pii e zhichige yaanh iwi.

I was not too little to go play bingo with my mother. I won $250.00, and my mother didn't win anything.

Je ne suis pas trop petit pour aller jouer au bingo avec ma mère. J'ai gagné 250 $, mais ma mère, elle, n'a rien gagné.

Gaawiin dash wiyii go ozaam ngii gaachiiwisii wii bibaa wiijiiwak ngashi bibaa taaget. Gaawiin ngashi gegoo gii pakinaagesiin, niin dash wiyii go niizhowaak shi naanamidana ngii pakinaagen.

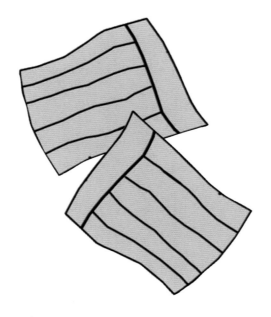

So I went to my father and complained. I said that I was definitely old enough to go fishing.

Je me suis plaint à mon père. J'ai dit que j'étais vraiment assez grand pour aller à la pêche.

Miidash gii dibaajimotawak noos. Ngii wiindamawaa geget go depiitizi yaanh ji bibaa gii goonkeyaanhmbaa geniin.

Father said that I could go out on the big boat on my next birthday. I went and told all my friends. Even Lucy Spence was impressed.

Mon père a dit qu'il m'emmènerait sur son gros bateau pour mon prochain anniversaire. Je l'ai dit à tous mes amis. Même Lucie Spence a été impressionnée.

Miidash noos gii wiidamawit gichi jiimaaning ji boozi yaanh pii dibishkaa yaanh. Kina ngii bibaa wiindamawaag nwiichkenhwenhik. Waa'aach go gewiin Lasii gii maamiikowendam pii waandamawag.

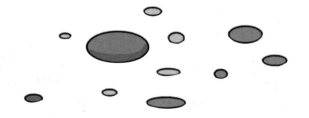

The day before my birthday, my father and uncle went out fishing.

La veille de mon anniversaire, mon père et mon oncle sont partis pêcher.

Giyaabi ngogiizhigak jibowaa dibishkaa yaanh, mii gii bibaa giigoonhkewaad noos miinawaa nzhishenh.

There was a big storm. They did not come back that night. I waited all the next day at the dock, and they did not come back. When it was nighttime, my mother came and took me home. She said that they were not coming back.

Une grosse tempête s'est levée. Ce soir-là, ils ne sont pas rentrés. Toute la journée du lendemain, j'ai attendu sur le quai, mais ils ne sont pas revenus. Quand la nuit est tombée, ma mère m'a ramené à la maison. Elle m'a dit qu'ils ne reviendraient plus.

Gii gichi nichiiwat dash. Gaawiin gii bipskaabiisiiwok e ninaakoshik. Gibegiizhik gaa waabang ngii baabiiyaak aazhoganing. Gaawiin go gii bipskaabiisiiwok. Miidash go e ninaagoshik, mii ngashi gii binaazhid, ngii nigiiwenik. Gaawiin wii pskaabiisiiwok gii kida.

I celebrated my birthday ten days after the funeral. I blew out the candles and didn't even open my presents. I got up from the table and walked down to the dock. Mr. Spence was going out on his fishing boat. I climbed in. He said, "Welcome aboard, Vincent," and started the motor.

J'ai fêté mon anniversaire dix jours après les funérailles. J'ai soufflé mes bougies, mais je n'ai pas ouvert mes cadeaux. Je suis sorti de table et je suis descendu jusqu'au quai. Monsieur Spence partait sur son bateau de pêche. J'y suis monté.

Midaaswigon gaa shkwaa bigidenjigeng mii gii minaajtoowaanh gii dibishkaa yaanh. Ngii aataweboodaadanan waaskonenjigaanhsan, gaawiin go waa'aach ngii baakanaziinan shkapijiganan. Ngii nibazigowii doopawining, aazhoganing ngii nizhigaadese. Mr. Spence megowaa zhiitaawitoon doo giigoonhke jiimaan. Ngii boozaandowe dash. "Ngichi inendam waabaminaan, Besaanh", gii kida, miidash gii maajiishkaatoot iwi jiimaan.

Then Lucy came running up and said that she wanted to come. Her father let her.

Lucie est arrivée en disant qu'elle voulait venir avec nous. Son père l'a laissée monter.

Lasii gii biijibatoot, gewiin wii bizhaa. Mii sa oosan gii bigidinigot wii bibaa wiijiiwigooyaang.

We caught a lot of fish.

Mr. Spence said that things come and things go, but the ocean and the people, we go on forever.

Nous avons pêché beaucoup de poissons.

Monsieur Spence a dit ceci :
— Les choses passent, mais l'océan et nous, nous serons là pour toujours.

Aapiji niibana giigoonhik ngii debinaanaanik.

Pane gegoo bidagoshinimigat miinawaa pane gegoo maajaamigat, maanda dash gichigomi miinawaa bemaadizijig, ga niyaamin pane, gii kida Mr. Spence.

About *The Ocean Goes on Forever*

Vincent, the boy in this story, is from a little reserve north of Prince Rupert, British Columbia, called Port Simpson. It's a fishing town with no road access, just below the border with Alaska. Salmon fishing is the main industry.

Vincent wrote me a letter in 1988 about the town and bingo and his telescope, and his father and uncle who both drowned. I wrote this story and sent it back to him. Lucy isn't real. I made up that part.

This book was first published in the Anishinaabemowin language – neat! I think having First Languages books is vital for group identity and pride.

Fiero Writing System
Syllable Chart

a (b<u>u</u>t)	i (k<u>i</u>t)	o (c<u>oo</u>k)	aa (s<u>aw</u>)	ii (tr<u>ee</u>)	oo (<u>o</u>pen)	e (p<u>e</u>t)

nh= nasal 'n'

SHORT VOWELS			LONG VOWELS			
a	i	o	aa	ii	oo	e
ba	bi	bo	baa	bii	boo	be
cha	chi	cho	chaa	chii	choo	che
da	di	do	daa	dii	doo	de
ga	gi	go	gaa	gii	goo	ge
ja	ji	jo	jaa	jii	joo	je
ka	ki	ko	kaa	kii	koo	ke
ma	mi	mo	maa	mii	moo	me
na	ni	no	naa	nii	noo	ne
pa	pi	po	paa	pii	poo	pe
sa	si	so	saa	sii	soo	se
sha	shi	sho	shaa	shii	shoo	she
ta	ti	to	taa	tii	too	te
wa	wi	wo	waa	wii	woo	we
ya	yi	yo	yaa	yii	yoo	ye
za	zi	zo	zaa	zii	zoo	ze
zha	zhi	zho	zhaa	zhii	zhoo	zhe

Robert Munsch

is Canada's most popular writer for children. His books are loved by kids across the country and around the world. But he didn't set out to be a writer. He started telling stories when he worked in daycare, and only began writing them down later. Almost all of his stories still start that way, so each one is based on a real kid he has met or who has sent him a letter. Each of the stories in this book is dedicated to the kid who inspired it.

Michael Martchenko

has always wanted to be an illustrator. He started out by copying out comic books, went to art college and worked in advertising. Then he met Robert Munsch and they collaborated on *The Paper Bag Princess* . . . and the rest is history. They have worked togther on 50 books and Michael has illustrated many more, some of which he also wrote. When he isn't painting children's books, Michael enjoys painting antique airplanes.

Jay Odjick

is an artist and writer from the Kitigan Zibi Anishinabeg Algonquin community. Jay comes from a comics background, having written and drawn his creator-owned graphic novel *KAGAGI: The Raven*, as well as producing and writing the *Kagagi* television series adaptation that will air on APTN. Jay has worked in illustration for years, in a variety of media including children's book illustration, comic books, and design for TV, film and games.